JOEY AND THE SHINING STAR

AN OWLEGORIES® TALE

CREATED BY THOMAS AND JULIE BOTO
ILLUSTRATED BY ANDREA WERNTZ

Joey was an active owl.
He was always on the move.

He had lots of big ideas.

"Follow me!" Joey shouted,
"I'll lead the way!"

But Violet did not follow Joey.

"Why are you going into the woods?" she asked. "That's not the way home."

Violet thought for a minute.

Gus thought for a minute.

"Okay Joey," Gus replied.

"I sure hope you know where you're going," said Violet.

So Joey and Violet and Gus marched into the woods.

They had been walking for awhile when they spotted a tall pine tree.

Joey hadn't seen this tree before. He began to wonder if he was going the right way.

But surely he hadn't made a mistake.
If they just kept walking, he knew he
could find the way.

"Hey!" Gus called out, "Did I ever tell you why Christmas trees are so bad at sewing?"

"No, why?" Violet asked.

"Because they're always losing their needles!"

Violet laughed at Gus' joke.

But Joey was not laughing.

"What's wrong, Joey?" Violet asked.

"Um . . . nothing's wrong," Joey replied.
"We're definitely not lost."

Gus leaned into Violet and whispered, "We're definitely lost, aren't we?"

But Joey kept marching. "It's this way, I know it!" he said.

The three friends kept walking.

And walking.

And walking.

"Hey, do you know why Christmas trees
are so bad at sewing?" Gus asked.

"Not now, Gus!" Violet said.
"Can't you see we're lost?!"

No matter how hard Joey tried,
he could NOT find his way out of the woods.

Before long, the three owl friends came back
to the same tall pine tree.

Joey hung his head.

Violet was right. They were lost.

And Joey knew it was his fault.

He knew what he needed to do.

"Gus? Violet?" Joey said quietly.

"Yes?" Gus and Violet replied.

"I'm sorry. I thought I knew a quick way to get home," said Joey. "But I don't know where we are. And now we're lost!"

"Hey, did I ever tell you what my grandma said about being lost?" Gus asked.

"Stop joking, Gus!" Violet said. "Can't you see we're lost?"

But Gus continued. "My grandma said if
I ever got lost on a clear night, to look for
the North Star. She said the North Star
would lead me toward home."

"That's right, Gus!" exclaimed Joey. "We can follow the star. Remember the Wise Men in the Christmas play? They followed a star to find their way to Jesus!"

"They wanted to celebrate the birth of Jesus. They walked and walked and walked, and God used the star to guide their way," said Violet.

"But there are so many stars in the sky," said Joey. "How will we know which one to follow?"

"I know where the North Star is!" Violet said.
"It's the brightest, whitest star in the sky."

The friends looked up into the wide night sky.

And there it was, twinkling and shining more brightly than all the other stars in the sky.

"Let's go!" shouted Joey.

So Joey, Violet, and Gus started marching home, but this time, the North Star was leading the way.

Joey whistled a little walking song,
and Gus and Violet hummed along.

Soon, they arrived safely back
to their neighborhood.

They were happy
to be home.

"I'm sorry I got us lost. Gus and Violet, thanks for helping us get home," Joey said.

"Sure thing, Joey!" Violet replied. "We saw some really great trees and learned something about God too!"

"Yep," said Joey. "Even when we're lost,
God guides us and helps us find our way!"

FAMILY TIME

"The heavens declare the glory of God; the skies proclaim the work of his hands."—Psalm 19:1 (NIV)

TALK ABOUT THE STORY:

> Christmas is a time to celebrate God's big love as we remember the birth of Jesus, God's greatest gift to us.

> When we look at the night sky, we see all the beautiful stars and the moon that God made. Like the Wise Men in the Christmas story, we know God is with us, guiding us and helping us find our way.

> God's love for us is as big as the universe.

> What can you see in the night sky tonight?

PRAY TOGETHER:

Thank you, God, for being our North Star, who helps us find our way. Amen.

MAKE SOMETHING:

1. Grab an empty toilet paper roll and piece of dark-colored paper.

2. Use a pencil to carefully poke holes in the paper.

3. Wrap one end of the toilet paper tube with the paper, securing it with a rubber band.

4. Now look through the tube toward a light. It will look like a starry sky!

5. Tonight, take the dark paper off the tube and bring the tube outside. Use it like a telescope and look for the North Star!

The Owlegories® brand and characters are the property of Spy House, LLC.

Created by Thomas and Julie Boto
Illustrated by Andrea Werntz
Designed by Mighty Media

First edition published 2017
Printed in the United States of America
23 22 21 20 19 18 17   1 2 3 4 5 6 7 8

ISBN: 9781506433042

Library of Congress Cataloging-in-Publication Data

Names: Boto, Thomas, author. | Boto, Julie, author. | Werntz, Andrea
    (Illustrator), illustrator.
Title: Joey and the shining star : an owlegories tale / created by Thomas and
    Julie Boto ; illustrated by Andrea Werntz.
Description: First edition. | Minneapolis, MN : Sparkhouse Family, 2017. |
    Summary: When three young owls get lost in the woods, one remembers
his grandmother's advice to follow the North Star, which reminds them all of
    the Christmas story. Includes "Family time" suggestions for discussion,
    prayer, and a craft.
Identifiers: LCCN 2017025933 | ISBN 9781506433042 (hardcover)
Subjects: | CYAC: Lost children--Fiction. | Stars--Fiction. |
    Christmas--Fiction. | Christian life--Fiction.
Classification: LCC PZ7.1.B676 Joe 2017 | DDC [E]--dc23 LC record available
at https://lccn.loc.gov/2017025933

VN0003466; 9781506433042; JUL2017

Sparkhouse Family
510 Marquette Avenue
Minneapolis, MN 55402
sparkhouse.org